NO BIG DEAL

Glenn Meganck

Illustrated by Jon Ward

Beachfront Kids

Beachfront Publishing
Boca Raton, Florida

Look for more Big Deal Books available now or coming soon!
Big Deal
Big Deal At The Center Of The Earth
Big Deal And The Fountain Of Youth
Big Deal Goes Batty
Big Deal, It's A Hurricane!

Contact Beachfront Publishing and our authors at:
Beachpub@aol.com

Library of Congress Cataloging-in-Publication Data
Meganck, Glenn. date
No Big Deal / by Glenn Meganck
p. cm.
Summary: Jimmy's alien friend Eon accidently makes him
invisible.
ISBN 1-892339-05-6 (pbk.)
[1. Extraterrestrial beings Fiction.] I. Ward, Jon, ill.
II. Title.
PZ7.M5137No 2000
[Fic]--dc21   99-36906
                                                         CIP

Printed in the United States of America 10 9 8 7 6 5 4 3 2 1

NO BIG DEAL

ONE

"Two points!"

The basketball went sailing in a high, smooth arc. Jimmy Deal watched it rise, admiring his shot. The bright orange ball hit the high backboard and bounced hard against the rim before jumping back wildly over his head.

The basketball kept on bouncing all the way across the street. "Rats," mumbled Jimmy, "thought I had that."

Jimmy heard a sharp, cough-like laugh from

behind and turned. It was his spooky, new neighbor, Vladimir Korsakov. Vladimir and his mother had moved into the empty house across the street a week ago. The kid had been nothing but a pain ever since.

"Nice shot, Red!" jeered Vlad.

Jimmy growled, "I told you before, my name is not Red."

Vlad shrugged. "You've got red hair, like a strawberry."

"And you've got black hair, like the bristles on the broom my mom uses to sweep the tile. Not to mention you are as pale as an onion or maybe even a zombie! What should I call you?"

"Watch it," cautioned Vlad.

"I know," laughed Jimmy, "how about black ghost?"

"Strawberry!"

"Just toss me back my basketball, will you, please?"

"Sure," said Vlad. The boy picked up the ball in his hands and spun it in the air. Then, instead of throwing the ball to Jimmy, Vlad tossed it over his shoulder and the orange ball landed near the front door of the Korsakov house.

"Very funny."

"I thought so," replied Vlad.

Jimmy took a step forward and into the street. "Come on, now, throw me back my ball!"

Vlad grinned and said, "Forget it. It's on my property. Finders keepers."

"Then I will come and get it myself," Jimmy said. He quickly crossed the street and marched up Vlad's drive. There was a low, white picket fence along the front with a gate blocking the sidewalk. Jimmy put his hand on the latch and heard a growl.

"Grwoof!"

A giant German shepherd came bounding from the side of the yard. He looked as big as a house. The dog ran to Vlad.

Vlad patted the beast's head. "Good, doggy," he said. The dog stuck out its tongue and licked Vlad's face. "Yes, good doggy," Vlad repeated.

Jimmy, who hadn't moved, said, "Hi, puppy," in as friendly a voice as he could muster.

"This is Hercules," Vlad explained. "Hercules doesn't like strangers, does he?" The big dog barked.

It was such a loud and forceful bark that Jimmy

felt his teeth shake. Jimmy let go of the gate latch. "This isn't over, Vlad. I want my ball back and I am going to get it!"

Vlad grinned and scratched Hercules between the ears. He said nothing.

Jimmy returned to his house determined to find a way to get his basketball back and no boy and his dog were going to stop him.

This was war!

TWO

"There's someone banging on the garage side door!" called Jimmy's mother. "Probably your friend, Ted."

"But I'm not dressed yet!" Jimmy hollered from his room. "I'm still in my underwear. Could you let him in, please?"

"All right," said Mrs. Deal.

Jimmy heard his mom head down the long hallway that led to the door off the garage. He heard her say good morning and recognized Ted's big mouth in reply. Boy, that kid was loud.

"Is Jimmy ready for school, Mrs. Deal?" Ted

asked.

"No, come inside and wait," Jimmy's mother replied. "You're early. How about something to eat?"

"That would be great." Ted licked his chops. He never, ever turned down food.

"Well, help yourself in the kitchen, Ted," Mrs. Deal told him. "I have to finish folding the laundry."

Ted passed Jimmy's door and gave it a rap. "Move it in there!" he shouted.

"Yeah, yeah, I'm coming!" said Jimmy, as he struggled to pull his favorite shirt over his wet hair. He was tired and mad. Jimmy had hardly slept for fretting over losing his basketball the day before. That Vladimir was going to pay.

It was a good thing that it was Friday, because that would give Jimmy the whole weekend to figure out a way to get his basketball back.

Ted headed for the kitchen and popped open the refrigerator. "Hmm," he muttered aloud. "Bread, cheese, apples. Juice!" He grabbed a carton of apple juice and set it on the counter.

"Hey, Mrs. Deal!" he shouted, "You got any crackers?"

"Bottom shelf, on the left, I think," Mrs. Deal answered from the laundry room. "Help yourself!"

"Thanks." Ted grabbed a mug from the draining tray by the kitchen sink and filled it within a hair's breadth of the rim with cold apple juice.

He pulled open the door to the bottom cupboard, rummaged around until he found a box of cinnamon graham crackers and ripped open a fresh pack. Ted set the box back in the cupboard and the crackers on the kitchen counter.

He needed a plate.

Ted was about to open one of the upper cabinets in search of the dishes when a blurry, dark shape caught his attention. "Hey!"

Ted inspected the counter closely. He saw nothing. A toaster, a blender, a roll of paper towels. Ted shrugged. It was probably nothing. He decided to use a paper towel for his crackers instead of looking for a dish. He yanked at the roll, tipping it over in the process.

"Argh!" Ted jumped back. Some ugly bug was scurrying from behind the paper towels and headed for the toaster! Ted picked up a cracker and threw it at the fast moving critter. It turned and headed back towards the paper towel dispenser.

No Big Deal

"Got you!" said Ted. He caught the bug in his hand and then quickly decided that might not have been the smartest thing he could do. For all he knew this could be some, stinging, venomous insect. Ted could swell up, turn purple like an eggplant and die!

He felt a pinprick. The thing was biting him! Ted looked around the kitchen for a place to put the deadly insect before it killed him. His eyes fell on the microwave oven over the stove.

Ted threw open the door to the microwave, tossed the insect inside, slammed the door just as quickly shut and pushed the timer for twenty minutes! "That'll fix you!"

"What's all the commotion?" shouted Jimmy, jogging out of his bedroom with his sneakers in his hands and the socks stuffed inside the shoes.

"Boy, are you going to thank me," said Ted quite proudly.

"What for?" said Jimmy suspiciously.

"I captured some big old bug that was lurking around on your counter."

"Bug? My mom hates bugs."

"Mine, too. And this one was gross. You should have seen it— big as your finger!"

"What did you do with it?" Jimmy asked. Maybe he should put his shoes on. There could be more of the insects crawling around. Bugs seemed to travel in bunches.

"Stuck it in the microwave," Ted replied. "Ought to be done anytime. Hungry?"

"Microwave? Yuck! Why didn't you toss him outside or at least in the trash can?" Jimmy could not imagine what his mother was going to think about a dead insect in her microwave. His mother seemed quite fond of her appliances. She kept them as clean and polished as trophies.

"I don't know," Ted said. He took a sip of apple juice and picked up one of his remaining crackers.

The microwave oven was still humming with nearly fifteen minutes to go.

"I wasn't thinking. I grabbed him and stuck him the first place I could think of. Darn thing was biting me or stinging me, who knows?" Ted inspected his hand for signs of forced entry.

Jimmy decided it was safe to sit down on the floor. He pulled one sock over his foot. "Better hurry before we're late for school."

"Yeah, you should have seen him. One ugly

No Big Deal

dude. Maybe I'll take it to school in a jar and show it to the science teacher, Mr. Cooper. He might know what kind of insect it is. Big and green. Ran upright, sort of like a person."

Jimmy half listened, as he laced up one shoe and started on the other.

"Had some sort of a star shaped head—"

"Did you say green?"

Ted nodded.

"Star shaped head? Kind of thick in the middle?"

"Yeah," Ted answered. "You seen one of the little buggers before, Jimmy?"

Jimmy shot to his feet and screamed, "EON!"

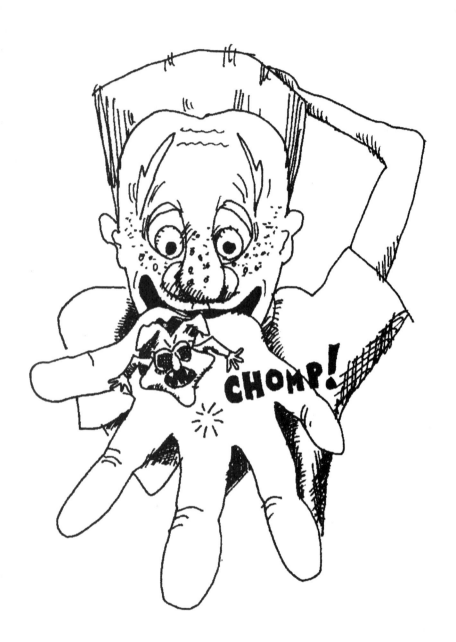

THREE

Jimmy raced across the kitchen floor and threw open the door to the microwave oven. A cloud of stinky smoke escaped into the air. "Oh, no!" shouted Jimmy, "You've killed him."

Jimmy waved the white smoke away with his hands while Ted looked on in wonder. Jimmy stuck his hand in the microwave and pulled out the tiny alien.

"Ouch! Hot!" Jimmy dropped Eon onto the pink granite counter top. The alien's hair was smoldering. He smelled like burnt toast.

Eon coughed and belched up a thick lungful of

smoke. "It's about time," he said in a raspy voice. Eon cleared his throat and checked his flesh. "Fortunately, we Ritarians are quite well adapted to high doses of radiation. All that space travel, you know."

The alien turned and looked angrily towards Ted. "It's having graham crackers thrown at us and being tossed in ovens that we most object to!"

"Hey, I'm only glad that you're okay, Eon. I didn't think I would ever see you again."

"You know this insect?" Ted asked.

"Insect!" said Eon. The tiny alien raised himself to his full height, which wasn't all that much. "I'll have you know that I am a Ritarian. Far, far more advanced than you, boy."

"Oh yeah?" said Ted. "Well, I didn't seem to have much trouble catching you, shorty. A few more minutes and you'd have been a roasted Ritarian."

"That does it," said Eon, reaching for his utility belt. "Now, where is that darn thing?"

Jimmy said, "Uh-oh."

"Uh-oh what?" teased Ted. "Bug boy gonna zap me?"

"Ted, I wouldn't—"

"Ooh, like I'm scared of you, Eon. Where did you meet this talking insect anyway, Jimmy? The zoo?"

Eon fumbled with a device on his belt in the shape of a tiny cannister.

"I found his spaceship one day and brought it home. Then Eon used his SIZER. That's a sonic integrated zippy energy ray, or something like that. It made me big, then little, then big again and little again. And then the Earth got blown up and—"

Ted was looking bugeyed at Jimmy. What the heavens was he talking about? And if Jimmy wasn't making this all up, Ted was in trouble!

"Aha!" Eon said, triumphantly. "Got it." He fumbled with the release catch on his belt and the device slipped into his hand. He aimed it menacingly at Ted.

Ted stepped back.

"Now, now, Eon," said Jimmy. "Temper, temper. Accidents happen."

"Accidents?" yelled Eon indignantly. "He threw me in the microwave and cooked me for five minutes!"

"Actually, I'd set the timer for twenty," said Ted, stepping in front of Jimmy.

No Big Deal

Eon shouted, "Twenty?! You could have killed me!"

"It was all your own fault."

"My fault?" said Eon.

"Yeah," continued Ted. "Scurrying around on the kitchen counter like some jungle insect. You look like some ugly, slimy, dirty little green thing from one of those National Geographic specials on the Amazon rain forest."

"Ted," warned Jimmy, "you're not helping things much."

"Well, it was his fault."

"Was not," said Eon.

"Was so."

"Was not!"

"Was so!"

"Was not, freckle face!"

"Bug head!"

"That does it," said Eon. He aimed the tiny gray cannister in his hand and fired.

"No!" Jimmy hollered. "Don't, Eon!" Jimmy tried to pull Ted back.

Ted ducked. . .and Jimmy got blasted!

FOUR

"Jimmy, where are you?"

Ted turned and shouted down at Eon, "What have you done to my best friend?"

"Well—"

Ted dropped to the ground and scanned the floor with his eyes. He gingerly patted the tiles with the palm of his hand. "What did you do? Shrink him to the size of an atom?"

"Hey," said Jimmy. "What's wrong with you, Ted? What are you screaming about?"

"Jimmy, is that you?"

"Of course, it's me. What are you doing on the

floor?"

Ted looked up. "I'm looking for you. Don't worry, I'll save you, Jimmy!"

"Save me from what? I'm right here, I'm fine. Quit joking and get up all ready, will you?"

Ted slowly stood and said, "I don't get it, Jimmy. I hear you. . .but—but I don't see you."

Jimmy laughed. "What are you talking about? I'm right here, as plain as the nose on your face. See?" Jimmy waved his arms. "Yikes! I can't see my arms!"

"Now look what you've done!" Eon said to Ted.

"Me?" Ted said indignantly. "My best friend is invisible and you're blaming me?"

"You shouldn't have ducked," Eon said.

"Oh, well excuse me," said Ted. "I guess I just didn't feel like getting blasted out of my shoes this morning."

"Yes, well maybe that is exactly what you need—"

"Excuse me," interrupted Jimmy, "But what about me? Eon, what have you done to me?"

"Well," said Eon with obvious hesitation. He cleared his throat. It still stung from the smoke he had inhaled. "I'm afraid you've been hit with

Negatizmo potion."

"Nega-what?" asked Jimmy.

"Negatizmo potion. It achieves the optimum balance between light absorption and reflection while allowing the molecules to maintain their basic structure."

"Hello," said Ted. "You mind speaking English?"

"Sorry," said Eon. "You're invisible, Jimmy."

Jimmy moaned. "Oh great."

"Wow," said Ted. "That's cool."

"Oh yeah? What do you think my mom is going to say? I don't think she is going to think it's so cool."

"Oh, right," answered Ted.

"Will it wash off?" Jimmy asked.

Eon rubbed his chin. "Hmmm, I don't believe so, kid. But give me some time, I might think of something to help. Maybe speed up the reappearing process."

"You'd better think of something fast," whispered Jimmy harshly, "Because I hear my mother coming!"

"Jimmy?" Mrs. Deal turned the corner carrying a basketful of folded, clean laundry. "Oh, hello,

Ted. Where's Jimmy?"

"Right here," said Ted. Jimmy kicked Ted in the shin. "Ouch! What did you—"

"Are you all right, Ted?"

"Yes, I've got a cramp, that's all." Ted rubbed his leg. "Jimmy is in his room, Mrs. Deal."

"You tell him to hurry or he'll be late for school," said Mrs. Deal.

"Yes, ma'am."

Mrs. Deal held the laundry basket against her hip with one arm. When she moved she almost smashed into Jimmy. Jimmy held his breath and sucked in his gut. Jimmy's mother pulled a couple of clean dish towels from the basket and hooked them over the oven door handle. "Don't you boys be late now," Mrs. Deal repeated as she left.

"Whew, that was close," said Ted.

"Yeah." Jimmy turned on the sink and washed his arms with hot, soapy water. "Nothing." He'd been hoping a good, old-fashioned scrubbing would do the trick and make him visible again.

Eon scurried out from behind the toaster where he had fled on Mrs. Deal's approach. "Well, I've got to be going, kid. If I think of anything to make you un-invisible, I'll give you a call."

No Big Deal

"Wait just one minute," said Jimmy, placing an invisible hand on the counter. Eon took a step and hit an invisible wall. It was Jimmy's hand. "You got me into this mess and you're going to get me out of it."

"Yeah," said Ted, "change him back already."

Eon extracted himself from Jimmy's invisible hand. "Sorry, kid. No can do. And even if I could, I don't have time. I only popped over to pick up a little something that I seem to have misplaced when I visited your little planet the last time."

"Jimmy, it's eight o'clock! Hustle it up!"

"Oh, no," said Jimmy. "Come on, Ted. We'll be late."

"But you're invisible. Don't you think people are going to notice? Don't you think Miss Market is going to notice?"

"We'll think of something, Ted." Jimmy turned to Eon. "Are you going to be here when I get back?"

"I suppose," said Eon. "I haven't had much luck finding my MAP yet."

"Map of what?"

"Not that kind of map, kid. My MAP. That's

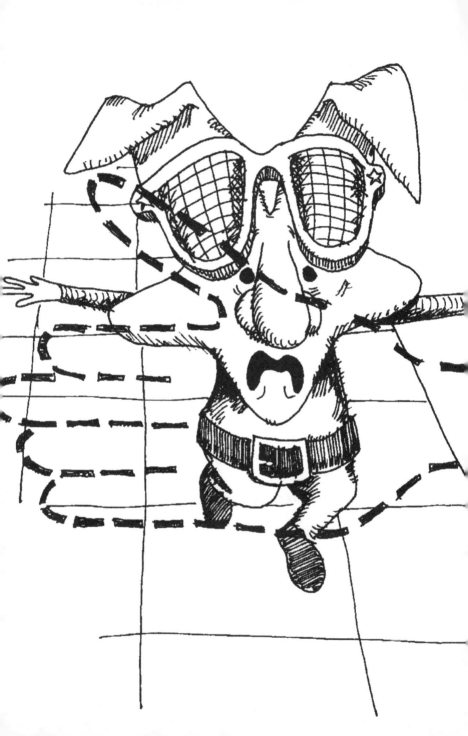

No Big Deal

magnification amplitude pulsater. It's my brother-in-law's actually. He keeps it on his Ride-A-Coach 2000. It helps lull us to sleep. Ritarians are notorious for having trouble falling asleep at night."

"You came back all this way for that?"

"Yes, I did. For one thing, my brother-in-law is fit to be tied. He insisted that I try to recover the MAP or buy him a new one. He says that I can't be trusted. My own sister's husband and he would not even let me borrow the Ride-A-Coach 2000 again. I had to get a rental!"

Jimmy had a bad feeling about this. It didn't seem to him that it would be worth returning millions of miles for something to help you sleep at night. Wouldn't it have been simpler for Eon to buy his brother-in-law a new MAP? "What's the other thing?"

"I was afraid you would ask me that," Eon said. "You see the MAP emits a frequency that helps Ritarians sleep. For humans, however, there is a negative side effect."

"What kind of side effect?" asked Ted.

"Prolonged exposure to the MAP can cause humans to develop gills."

"Gills?" Ted said.

Glenn Meganck

Jimmy said, "You mean like a-a—"
"Fish," said Eon.

FIVE

Jimmy groaned, "So, not only am I invisible, but now I'm going to be an invisible fish—"

"Yeah, me too," said Ted. He rubbed his face and neck, searching for gills or any signs of fish-like development. "I don't want to be a fish. I don't even like to take baths!"

"Yes, by the smell of you I would say that's quite obvious," commented Eon.

"Listen, you—"

"That's enough!" said Jimmy. "My mom's going to hear you both. Now, Eon, how long will it take you to get back this MAP of yours?"

"Should be a snap, kid." Eon slapped his utility belt. "Brought along an audio analyzer." He pulled another device from his belt. It looked like a miniature portable radio. "With this baby, I can track the signal that the MAP is emitting. I'll have it back in a jiffy."

Jimmy said, "Well, at least that's some good news."

"You betcha." Eon flipped open the cover of the audio analyzer. "Uh-oh. . ."

"Again he uh-ohs," said Ted.

"What's wrong?" asked Jimmy.

"The electronic circuitry has been fried. Gee, I wonder how that could have happened?" Eon said, looking directly at Ted.

"Hey, don't blame me. I thought you were a bug."

"Can't you get it to work at all?" Jimmy asked.

"Nope, I'm afraid it's useless." Eon stuck the melted audio analyzer back on his belt. "Looks like I'm going to have to scout around and visually try to locate the MAP. But don't worry."

"Why not?" asked Ted.

"Because," answered Eon, "even if you earthlings do turn into fish — there's plenty of room in

the ocean for all of you!"

"Very funny," said Ted.

"Listen," said Jimmy. "We've got to go to school, but today is Friday. So after school, Ted and I will help you look, Eon. I've got something I want to look for myself."

"Like what?" asked Ted.

"My basketball." Jimmy nudged Eon. "What does this MAP look like, anyway?"

Eon shrugged. "Not much to it. It's round and big and gold colored."

"How big?"

"About like this, kid." The little Ritarian held his hands apart.

"That's only about the size of a penny!" Ted exclaimed.

"Yes, come to think of it, it is rather shaped like one of your coins. Flat as a dime, I'd say. But there's a hole near the top from which the special frequencies are emitted."

"But, that's not big at all. Oh boy, are we in trouble! There are sharks in the ocean! We'll be eaten!"

"Relax," said Jimmy. "We'll find the MAP."

"Sure, you kids go to school. I've got every-

No Big Deal

thing under control." Eon turned to Jimmy. "Give me a lift to the door, will you?"

Jimmy scooped Eon up in his invisible hand. They headed out the garage. Jimmy's mother was still in her bedroom. "Bye, Mom!"

"Wait, come give me a kiss!" shouted Mrs. Deal.

"Can't! I'll be late for school!" Jimmy answered. There was no way he could let his mother see him like this, or rather not see him!

Jimmy set Eon down on the front lawn. "You going to be okay?"

"I'm not a baby, kid."

"Oh, yeah, I keep forgetting." Jimmy and Ted hopped on their bikes. "See ya!"

Jimmy pushed off down the sidewalk.

"Wait!" shouted Ted.

Jimmy turned and said, "What's wrong?"

"What's wrong? There's a bicycle riding down the sidewalk all by itself. That's what's wrong."

"Oh, that's right." Jimmy rolled his bike back to the garage. "You'll have to give me a ride, Ted. Scoot over."

Jimmy squeezed onto the seat behind Ted. Ted pushed off and the bike wobbled unsteadily down

the drive.

"Good luck, Eon."

There was no reply.

"Eon?" There was no sign of the little alien.

"Fast little bugger, isn't he?" said Ted.

"Yeah," replied Jimmy. "I only hope Mr. Butterman's cat doesn't eat him." Mr. Butterman, his next-door neighbor, had a fat tabby cat named Egbert who was always chasing such things as lizards and beetles. The little Ritarian just might find himself being batted about like a cat toy. Hopefully, Eon could take care of himself like he said.

Huffing and puffing from the extra weight, Ted pulled into the schoolyard of Ocean Palm Elementary School. Ted pushed his bicycle into the bike rack and locked it up.

As they walked up to the classroom, Ted asked Jimmy, "Do you have any idea how you're going to explain being invisible to Miss Market?"

"None." Jimmy dodged to avoid being run over by a kindergartner and her mother. "Did you see that, they almost ran into me. What's with everybody today? Can't they be more careful?"

"You're invisible, Jimmy. They can't see you." A teacher walked by and noticed Ted who appeared to be talking to himself. Ted shut up, smiled and kept on walking.

The boys took their seats near the back of Miss Market's classroom. She was already calling the roll. Soon it was their turn.

"Ted Ledbetter?"

"Present," Ted replied.

"And Jimmy Deal—" Miss Market looked around the room. "Jimmy?"

"He's, uh—" mumbled Ted.

"Present!" shouted Jimmy. His muffled voice had come from behind the restroom door.

Ted sighed with relief. "He's in the bathroom, Miss Market."

Miss Market nodded and checked Jimmy Deal's name off on the daily roll. "Now, there's just time for a quick slide show about dinosaurs before we leave for the museum." Miss Market dimmed the lights. In the darkness, Jimmy quietly snuck back to his seat.

SIX

Ted spoke, "There's the Museum of Science."

"I'm invisible, not blind," whispered Jimmy. "I can see it."

"Oh, right," said Ted. No one paid any attention to the empty space next to the window in aisle twenty-one of the big yellow school bus. It was a good thing too, because that empty space was Jimmy. Ted sat beside him.

The bus pulled up the curved drive at the entrance of the long, low science museum building and came to a stop.

The kids burst out and Miss Market had her

hands full keeping them together and organized. She clapped her hands. "Now, class, remember, we stay together and use the buddy system. Everyone pair up." Miss Market counted heads. She came up one short. "Where's Jimmy?"

Jimmy whispered in Ted's ear. "Tell her I ran inside to use the bathroom."

"Jimmy had to go potty, Miss Market," Ted told his teacher.

All his classmates laughed. "What did you say potty for?" Jimmy said.

"Sorry, it just came out," Ted mumbled, trying not to move his lips. It wasn't easy.

"You mean he's in the bathroom again? Jimmy's not sick, is he?"

"No, ma'am. I think it's only something he ate. I believe his mother cooked up something weird for breakfast."

"Weird?"

"Yeah, she's always trying new things. Today I think it was uh—" Ted struggled for something to say.

Jimmy wondered why his best friend couldn't keep his mouth shut.

"Green eggs and Spam."

His classmates all laughed again.

"You mean green eggs and ham?

"Yeah, that's what I meant."

"Green Eggs and Ham? That's a book by Dr. Seuss, Ted," answered Miss Market.

"Really? Well that must be where Jimmy's mother got the idea. She's always looking at cookbooks."

"It's not a—" Miss Market shook her head. "You run inside and make sure Jimmy is all right. Then I expect you both back here in exactly two minutes. We'll be at the Dinosaur Walk. Come along, class."

Miss Market organized the rest of the class in a line, marching two by two off toward the Dinosaur Walk.

"It's going to be a long day," groaned Ted. "What are we going to do now, Jimmy? Jimmy?" Ted did a three-sixty. He groped the air. "Jimmy?"

"Over here!"

Ted turned. The sound had come from up the steps leading to the museum. "Where are you?"

"By the gift shop."

Ted ran up the steps and ran into Jimmy.

No Big Deal

"Oooph! Sorry."

"Never mind," said Jimmy. "Look in the window."

Ted gazed through the window of the museum gift shop. There were all kinds of cool things, t-shirts, glow in the dark moon balls, rubber bugs and lizards, kites, exotic looking rocks, gyros, kaleidoscopes. "Yeah, cool. They've even got fossils. I've always wanted a real fossil—"

"No," said Jimmy. "Costumes. They've got dinosaur costumes!"

"Yes, I see them. They're okay, but I think I'll buy some fossils—"

"No, don't you get it, Ted? I can wear the costume and no one will know that I'm invisible."

"Hey, yeah."

"Have you got any money?"

"My mom gave me a twenty dollar bill because it was all she had. I'm not supposed to spend it all though, except for an emergency."

Jimmy said, "This is an emergency. Go inside and see how much it is."

Ted agreed. Moments later he came out carrying a museum bag. "I got you the raptor."

"Terrific." Jimmy pulled Ted behind a bush

near the side of the museum. "Help me get this thing on."

SEVEN

"I feel silly riding around with a dinosaur on my bike," Ted commented as he pedaled back to his best friend's house.

"How do you think I feel?" asked Jimmy. "I'll never be able to live this down at school."

Jimmy had been stuck wearing the raptor suit all day. To make sure it didn't come off, he'd bent the zipper pull on the inside. Not even Miss Market had been able to budge it. So she'd had no choice but to let him keep the costume on.

And it was hot. Not to mention everybody in his class made fun of him. Even Miss Market

47

laughed and told him how cute he looked climbing on the bus in a dinosaur suit.

But what choice did he have? Jimmy gritted his teeth and kept the costume on all day long.

And it was a long day. . .

Eon waved to Ted as he coasted up the driveway. "My goodness! What's happened? Jimmy, is that you?" Eon looked quite startled.

"Yes," said Jimmy. "And now I've turned into a dinosaur and it's all your fault!"

Ted stopped his bike with his feet and dropped the kickstand.

"Gee, kid, I'm sorry. I've got a transmutational device here somewhere. Let me see—" The tiny alien searched his utility belt. "I know I packed it. Don't worry, Jimmy. A couple of shots ought to do the trick."

"Wait!" cried Jimmy. He had to stop the joke before Eon could do him any more harm. "I'm kidding." Jimmy turned around and pointed at the zipper in back. "See? It's a costume."

"Oh, very good, very good," said Eon.

Ted laughed. "Got you!"

"Can we get serious, please?" asked Eon.

Jimmy shook his head up and down. Of course, being in a dinosaur costume it looked sort of ridiculous. So, of course, Ted laughed again. Really, he couldn't help himself.

"Well, if that's how you feel," said Eon. "If you'd really rather be fish—"

"Okay," said Jimmy. "Sorry."

"Me too." Ted looked solemn.

"Can you make me visible again?"

"Uh, no," admitted Eon, "but I'm working on it." Actually, he had no idea how to make Jimmy visible again. "I have good news though," said the Ritarian. "I have located the missing MAP."

"Where?" Jimmy asked.

Eon pointed to the house across the street. "There."

Jimmy's eyes were drawn to an upstairs window. "And that's my basketball!" Vlad had stuck Jimmy's basketball in his bedroom window. The nerve of the kid!

"Earlier this afternoon, I spotted one of your adult Earth creatures, a female, I believe, with coal black hair, enter that structure. The MAP was attached to a gold bracelet on her wrist along with many other trinkets, including a golden apple, a

dog, a cat, a thimble, a tiny pair of scissors—" Eon rubbed his hands together and said with envy, "I could really use those. You know how hard it is to get a good, sharp pair of scissors on Ritar?"

"That sounds like Vlad's mother," Jimmy replied. "She's got a charm bracelet. I noticed it when she introduced herself to my mom the day they moved in."

"What's your ball doing up there?" asked Ted.

Jimmy explained to Eon and Ted how Vladimir had gotten hold of his basketball and refused to return it.

"I'm going up there right now and get it," said Jimmy bravely.

"Wait," said Eon. "The most important thing is that I recover the MAP and disable it before you all turn into fish. Does a ball really matter?"

Jimmy thought of his autographed basketball. "It matters to me."

Ted said, "But what about the dog, Hercules?"

"Maybe he's sleeping."

"That brings me to my plan," announced Eon. "I suggest we wait until dark and creep into the house. I shall retrieve the MAP and you and Ted can get your basketball, Jimmy."

No Big Deal

"But what do I do until then? My mom is never going to let me wear this dinosaur suit the rest of the day. Especially not during supper."

Ted snapped his fingers. "That's easy. Tell her you're spending the night at my house!"

"Hey, yeah!" agreed Jimmy.

"Then all we have to do is hide out until it gets dark. Come on," said Ted. "We'll call your mother from my house."

EIGHT

"Okay," whispered Ted, "so how do we get inside?"

The two boys were hiding behind a big bush near the Korsakov's front door. Eon stood between them. Jimmy had shucked his raptor costume and was invisible once again.

Jimmy looked all around. "I don't see any open windows."

"Maybe the door isn't locked," Ted suggested.

"Yeah, that's possible," Eon said.

"Go try it, Jimmy," Ted said.

"Me! Why me?"

No Big Deal

"Because you're invisible. Nobody is going to see you anyway."

"Oh, right," said Jimmy. He hated it when Ted was right. He crept out of the bushes and tried the polished brass handle. It didn't budge.

"Look out!" whispered Ted. "It's Mrs. Korsakov!"

Jimmy turned towards the street. Mrs. Korsakov was striding up the sidewalk with the big dog, Hercules, straining at the leash. Vlad's mother reached over and opened the front gate.

"Yikes!" shouted Eon. "Lift me up! Lift me up! That beast could swallow me whole!"

Ted picked Eon up in his hand and stuffed him in his front shirt pocket. "Shh!" he whispered.

Jimmy stood in front of the door and held his breath. Hercules was barking madly now.

"Stop, Hercules," scolded Mrs. Korsakov. "What ever has gotten into you?" The German shepherd growled and bared his teeth in Jimmy's direction. One good bite could take out a whole kneecap! "You see something? A mouse? A snake?"

Hercules growled some more. Mrs. Korsakov's grip on the leash loosened a bit as she reached for her house keys. Gratefully, it didn't take her long to turn the key in the lock. As she opened the door and led Hercules inside, Jimmy slipped in behind her.

"Come on, Herc," said Mrs. Korsakov, "I've got some nice biscuits for you."

Jimmy leaned against the door and wiped invisible sweat from his forehead. His heart was thumping like a tom-tom. But he was inside!

He waited until Mrs. Korsakov had disappeared in the kitchen then inched open the front door. "Come on," he whispered.

Ted crept inside with Eon in his pocket. "Where's the dog?"

"Stay here," Jimmy said. "I'll go check."

Jimmy tiptoed down the hall in the direction Vlad's mom had taken. Across the kitchen he saw her giving Hercules a big bone.

She led Hercules into the laundry room where his dog bowl lay on the floor and said, "Now, you eat your yummy bone and be a good doggy." Mrs. Korsakov petted Hercules between the ears and shut the safety gate attached to the doorway.

Jimmy stuck his tongue out at the dog, though of course the pooch couldn't see it. Too bad,

No Big Deal

Jimmy hadn't appreciated the dumdum scaring him like that.

Jimmy heard Mrs. Korsakov thumping lightly up the stairs and ran back to his friends. "The coast is clear. She's got the dog locked up in the laundry room, let's go!"

Jimmy grabbed Ted's hand. "Hold on to me so you'll know where I am." Jimmy led them down the foyer. He stopped when he heard television sounds coming from what must be the family room. "Uh-oh, somebody's in there." Jimmy peaked around the corner and saw the top of Vlad's head over a chair. "It's dumb old Vlad."

"We'd better go another way," Ted said.

"There is no other way. The stairs is across the other side of the family room. Get down on your hands and knees and crawl. Vlad's so absorbed in the t.v. that he'll never notice us if we're quiet."

Ted gulped and nodded. He was beginning to wonder what he was doing here. Then he remembered about being turned into a fish and decided to stay. Some things were worth fighting for.

Jimmy tugged at Ted's arm and said, "Come on."

"You know, kid," said Eon, "it would be a lot

simpler if I just blasted everybody. Why I've got a little gizmo here that can—"

"No!" Jimmy said. "No blasting. Now, come on." He pulled Ted and Eon along the tiled floor. Slowly they neared the chair. Vlad barely moved. He was sitting there watching some mindless sitcom and eating a peanut butter sandwich.

"That's it!" shouted Eon.

Ted slapped a finger over the little alien's big mouth and gave him a dirty look. "You're going to get us caught!" he mouthed.

"What's it?" Jimmy whispered.

Eon pried Ted's yucky finger off of his lips. "Never mind, I'll tell you later— If I can remember." Eon and Ted made ugly faces at one another and Jimmy dragged them forward.

"Once we get past the chair it's only a couple of feet to the stairs. We should be okay once we get there."

"Yeah," Ted said softly, "unless Vlad's mom decides to come down the stairs at the same time as we're going up."

Jimmy didn't like to even think about that.

NINE

"This looks like Vlad's room," whispered Jimmy. There was a soccer poster tacked to the outside of the door. He peaked inside. The room was empty. And messy!

That kid was something. Jimmy's mom would never let him get away with a room this messy. Boy, was Vlad lucky!

Jimmy noticed a light coming from a room further up the hall. Mrs. Korsakov must be in there. Jimmy's basketball was still in the bedroom window where Vlad had stuck it. "You run in and get it, Ted. I'll watch the door."

No Big Deal

"Okay," replied Ted.

"Wait," Eon said. "Put me down so I can retrieve the MAP from the female."

"How are you going to do that?" Jimmy asked.

Eon shrugged. "I'm so small, she'll probably never notice me. Don't worry," the little alien said with utmost confidence.

Ted set Eon on the ground and the Ritarian began jogging up the hall towards the light in Mrs. Korsakov's room. "I'll get the ball, Jimmy."

Ted picked up the basketball, spun it in his hands and passed it through the open door where it banged loudly against the wall. It knocked two framed pictures to the ground. The sharp sound of breaking glass split the air.

The basketball bounced off the hard floor and thumped down the stairs.

"What did you do that for?" cried Jimmy in dismay.

"I was passing it to you! You said you were going to be watching the door, so I just assumed you'd be standing there."

Ted looked around Vlad's bedroom, trying desperately to figure out where Jimmy was. It's a pain trying to have a conversation with somebody

who is invisible and even harder to have an argument with one.

"Well, I moved," said Jimmy. "I'm over here by the bed!"

They heard a scream. It was a woman's scream.

Jimmy said, "Quick, Ted, run! You've got to get out of here before Mrs. Korsakov catches you!"

Ted gulped and ran out into the hall. He took the steps three at a time.

"A bug!" shouted Mrs. Korsakov.

Jimmy watched as Mrs. Korsakov came running out from her room wielding a big yellow fly swatter in one hand and a can of bug spray in the other.

Eon was screaming.

Vlad's mother was screaming. She swung at Eon and missed. Mrs. Korsakov aimed the bug spray. Another step and she'd have him. She leaped into the air in an attempt to squash the little alien. Eon had the MAP in his hands.

Jimmy jerked the hall rug and Eon popped into the air.

Jimmy grabbed Eon and bolted.

Mrs. Korsakov slipped on the waxed floor, tumbled and came up running. "I'll get you, you ugly little cockroach!" she shouted.

Vlad's mother swung the fly swatter like a mace. It missed Eon, but hit Jimmy square in the face. "Ouch!"

Vlad's mother couldn't believe her ears. Had the little bug said ouch?

She stopped just long enough for Jimmy to carry Eon down the stairs and out the front door. He didn't even slow down as he raced past Vlad who, through all the commotion, hadn't even turned his head from the television.

Jimmy only hoped that Ted had had the sense to get out of the house too!

Jimmy jumped over the picket fence and collapsed, panting on his front lawn.

Eon struggled out of Jimmy's grasp and lay on the grass next to him. "Boy, kid, it would have been simpler to let you all turn into fish." Eon paused to catch his breath. "Especially that crazy dame."

Across the street, Mrs. Korsakov threw open the front door and held up her fly swatter like a battle sword. Finding no dragons or bugs to slay she soon retreated inside.

A sound came from behind. Jimmy pushed himself up and turned.

Glenn Meganck

Ted stood bouncing Jimmy's special autographed basketball in the driveway. He was grinning. "Anybody care to shoot some hoops?"

TEN

"You got it!" shouted Jimmy.

"Yep, no problem," said Ted. "I'd toss it to you, if I could see you."

Jimmy snatched the ball out of Ted's hands and aimed for the basketball hoop. Swish! "All right!"

"Wow," Ted said. "Being invisible, Jimmy, you could be like the secret weapon on a basketball team."

"You could be right," said Jimmy, bouncing the ball and taking another shot. "But I'd still rather be my old self again." He looked at Eon who stood on the sidelines.

"Sorry, kid," said the little alien. All he could see was the spinning orange ball. "Wish I could help."

Ted asked, "Isn't there anything you can do?"

Eon scratched his head. "I know there's something. If only I could remember."

"Something that could make me visible again?"

Eon nodded. "If I think of it I'll give you a buzz. In the meantime, I'd better get this MAP back to Ritar before you're all sprouting fins. Get my Rent-A-Coach 1000 for me, will you, kid? It's under the kitchen sink behind the cleanser."

Jimmy set the ball down on the driveway and ran inside.

"Come on," said Ted, "try to remember. Was it one of your gizmos?"

Eon shook his head no.

"A pill?"

"No."

"A shot?"

"Nope."

Jimmy returned with Eon's ship and set it on the ground beside the alien. Eon pushed a button on his belt and the door to his spaceship slowly opened. "That dinosaur suit of yours does give me

an idea though, Jimmy."

"What's that?"

"I could have my tailor back on Ritar make a custom Jimmy suit for you. His name is Bikbak and he's the best. All I have to do is return with a picture of what you look like and he can make a costume that looks just like you."

"You mean I'd have to wear a costume of myself?"

"Sure, what do you think?"

"That's crazy," said Ted.

"What happens when I grow?"

"Hmmm." Eon scratched his starry head. "I hadn't thought of that."

"Aw, nuts," urged Ted, "isn't there anything else you can do?"

"Nuts!" Eon threw his little arms up in the air. "That's it! Remember when we were in that crazy dame's house and sneaking behind the chair?"

"And you shouted and nearly got us caught—" Ted said. "Sure, we remember. What about it?"

"That kid, Vlad. He was eating an Arachis hypogaea sandwich!"

"Huh?" said Jimmy and Ted in unison.

"Arachnid? That means spider," said Jimmy.

No Big Deal

"Gross!" Ted replied.

"Not arachnid, Arachis. Let me search my Earth index." Eon grabbed a device that looked like a palmtop computer and pushed some keys. "Peanut butter."

Jimmy looked at Ted. Ted tried to look at Jimmy, but of course he was invisible!

"What's peanut butter got to do with anything, Eon? Did Mrs. Korsakov slap you upside the head with that fly swatter? Or is breathing Earth air making you nutty?"

Eon laughed. "Oh, not me, kid. You!"

"I don't know," whispered Ted, in what he hoped was Jimmy's direction, "but I say the little bug has gone buggy!"

"I heard that!" said Eon. "Now, listen, Jimmy. The chemical composition of the peanut is very close to the composition of the invisibility ray antidote."

"You're telling me that all I have to do is eat a peanut butter sandwich and I'll be cured? That's great! Come on, Ted! Snack time!"

"Wait," said Eon. "Eating won't work. After all, the invisibility ray has altered your exterior molecules. The antidote works the same way."

"I don't get it," Jimmy said. He picked up his basketball and tossed it towards the backboard. It struck the rim and fell through the net.

Ted stuck out his foot to keep the ball from rolling into the Rent-A-Coach 1000. The last thing he wanted was for Eon to be stuck on Earth with that MAP, waiting for some alien to pick him up on a rescue mission, by which time he and the rest of humanity would all be fishes.

Eon leaned across his spacecraft. "Listen, kid," he said, "here's what you have to do—"

ELEVEN

"This is so gross," said Jimmy.

Ted tried hard not to laugh. "You look like one of those stinky monsters that we saw before," he said, referring to the time he and Jimmy had been trapped underground by crazy Miss Lucy and her eyeball sucking sand creatures.

Poor Jimmy was covered head to toe in peanut butter. "Thanks for bringing over all the peanut butter at your house, Ted."

"No problem, Jimmy. Mom buys it at that bulk warehouse."

Jimmy nodded. He knew the place well.

No Big Deal

"And I told my mom that we were going to spend the night at your house after all. I sure hope Eon knows what he's talking about making you cover yourself with gooey peanut butter like this."

"He does," said Jimmy, expressing more confidence than he felt in the little Ritarian. According to Eon, all Jimmy had to do was keep himself covered in peanut butter for twelve hours and the effects of the invisibility ray would wear off.

Eon was probably halfway to Ritar right now so his plan had better work.

"Quick!" said Ted. "I hear your mom coming!"

Jimmy shut off the bedroom light. Ted dove inside his sleeping bag on the floor. Jimmy hopped under the covers and moaned. Crawling into bed coated with sticky peanut butter. How disgusting!

Mrs. Deal opened Jimmy's bedroom door. Light from the hallway filled the room. "You boys in bed already?"

"Yes, Mom." Jimmy had the covers over his head. Ted waved at Mrs. Deal from his sleeping bag.

Mrs. Deal sniffed the air. "It smells like peanuts in here. Have you boys been eating in bed?"

"No, Mom."

"Well, it sure smells like peanuts."

"It's the Martian air," explained Jimmy. "We're on Mars, Mom."

"Oh, I see," said Mrs. Deal with a smile. "Would you like me to read to you?"

"No, thanks. I'm really tired. We both are," said Jimmy.

Ted nodded in agreement.

"All right then. Pull down the covers so I can kiss you goodnight."

"I can't, Mom," Jimmy said, hoping desperately that his mother would go along with what he was about to say. After all, how could he possibly explain being under the sheets covered in peanut butter? "I'm under the Astrodome of Mars. If I lift the cover, the seal will be destroyed and I'll suffocate and the Martians will get me!"

Mrs. Deal chuckled. "Oh, I understand. Good night, Ted."

"Good night, Mrs. Deal."

She patted the bedcovers. "See you in the morning, dear," Mrs. Deal said, shutting Jimmy's door.

"I sure hope so," whispered Jimmy. "I sure hope so."